Four Short Stories

The Miller's Daughter

by

Émile Zola

Double9 BOOKS

Four Short Stories
The Miller's Daughter
by Émile Zola

ISBN: 978-93-62204-01-1

Published by

DOUBLE 9 BOOKS
2/13-B, Ansari Road
Daryaganj, New Delhi – 110002
info@double9books.com
www.double9books.com
Tel. 011-40042856

ABOUT THE AUTHOR

French author, journalist, dramatist, and founder of the naturalism literary movement, Émile Zola also wrote plays. He played a significant role in both Alfred Dreyfus' exoneration and the political liberalisation of France. Dreyfus had been wrongfully charged and imprisoned as an army commander. In 1901 and 1902, Zola was a candidate for the Nobel Prize in Literature. Zola was born in Paris on April 2, 1840, to François Zola and Émile Aubert. Before becoming a writer, he was a law student who twice failed the baccalaureate. In his formative years, Zola produced a large number of short stories, essays, plays, and novels. Hachette fired Zola from his position as director of the Paris Opera in 1864 after the release of his scandalous autobiographical book La Confession de Claude (1865), which attracted the attention of the authorities. Zola became a citizen of France in 1862. He met the seamstress Éléonore-Alexandrine Meley, also known as Gabrielle, in 1865, and she eventually became his mistress. On September 29, 1902, Francois Zola died from carbon monoxide poisoning brought on by a poorly ventilated chimney. At the time of his death, he was working on the sequel to his recently published book Vérité, which is about the Dreyfus trial.

CONTENTS

CHAPTER I
THE BETROTHAL 7

CHAPTER II
THE ATTACK ON THE MILL 13

CHAPTER III
THE FLIGHT 21

CHAPTER IV
A TERRIBLE EXPERIENCE 28

CHAPTER V
THE RETURN OF THE FRENCH 35

CHAPTER I
THE BETROTHAL

Père Merlier's mill, one beautiful summer evening, was arranged for a grand fête. In the courtyard were three tables, placed end to end, which awaited the guests. Everyone knew that Francoise, Merlier's daughter, was that night to be betrothed to Dominique, a young man who was accused of idleness but whom the fair sex for three leagues around gazed at with sparkling eyes, such a fine appearance had he.

Père Merlier's mill was pleasing to look upon. It stood exactly in the center of Rocreuse, where the highway made an elbow. The village had but one street, with two rows of huts, a row on each side of the road; but at the elbow meadows spread out, and huge trees which lined the banks of the Morelle covered the extremity of the valley with lordly shade. There was not, in all Lorraine, a corner of nature more adorable. To the right and to the left thick woods, centenarian forests, towered up from gentle slopes, filling the horizon with a sea of verdure, while toward the south the plain stretched away, of marvelous fertility, displaying as far as the eye could reach patches of ground divided by green hedges. But what constituted the special charm of Rocreuse was the coolness of that cut of verdure in the most sultry days of July and August. The Morelle descended from the forests of Gagny and seemed to have gathered the cold from the foliage beneath which it flowed for leagues; it brought with it the murmuring sounds, the icy and concentrated shade of the woods. And it was not the sole source of coolness: all sorts of flowing streams gurgled through the forest; at each step springs bubbled up; one felt, on following the narrow pathways, that there must exist subterranean lakes which pierced through beneath the moss and availed themselves of the smallest crevices at the feet of trees or between the rocks to burst forth in crystalline fountains. The whispering voices of these brooks were so numerous and so loud that they drowned the song of the bullfinches. It was like some enchanted park with cascades falling from every portion.

Below the meadows were damp. Gigantic chestnut trees cast dark shadows. On the borders of the meadows long hedges of poplars exhibited in lines their rustling branches. Two avenues of enormous plane trees stretched across the fields toward the ancient Château de Gagny, then a mass of ruins. In this constantly watered district the grass grew to an extraordinary height. It resembled a garden between two wooded hills, a natural garden, of which the meadows were the lawns, the giant trees marking the colossal flower beds. When the sun's rays at noon poured straight downward the shadows assumed a bluish tint; scorched grass slept in the heat, while an icy shiver passed beneath the foliage.

And there it was that Père Merlier's mill enlivened with its ticktack a corner of wild verdure. The structure, built of plaster and planks, seemed as old as the world. It dipped partially in the Morelle, which rounded at that point into a transparent basin. A sluice had been made, and the water fell from a height of several meters upon the mill wheel, which cracked as it turned, with the asthmatic cough of a faithful servant grown old in the house. When Père Merlier was advised to change it he shook his head, saying that a new wheel would be lazier and would not so well understand the work, and he mended the old one with whatever he could put his hands on: cask staves, rusty iron, zinc and lead. The wheel appeared gayer than ever for it, with its profile grown odd, all plumed with grass and moss. When the water beat upon it with its silvery flood it was covered with pearls; its strange carcass wore a sparkling attire of necklaces of mother-of-pearl.

The part of the mill which dipped in the Morelle had the air of a barbaric arch stranded there. A full half of the structure was built on piles. The water flowed beneath the floor, and deep places were there, renowned throughout the district for the enormous eels and crayfish caught in them. Below the fall the basin was as clear as a mirror, and when the wheel did not cover it with foam schools of huge fish could be seen swimming with the slowness of a squadron. Broken steps led down to the river near a stake to which a boat was moored. A wooden gallery passed above the wheel. Windows opened, pierced irregularly. It was a pell-mell of corners, of little walls, of constructions added too late, of beams and of roofs, which gave the mill the aspect of an old, dismantled citadel. But ivy had grown; all sorts of clinging plants stopped the too-wide chinks and threw a green cloak over the ancient building. The young ladies who passed by sketched Père Merlier's mill in their albums.

On the side facing the highway the structure was more solid. A stone gateway opened upon the wide courtyard, which was bordered to the right and to the left by sheds and stables. Beside a well an immense elm covered half the courtyard with its shadow. In the background the building displayed the four windows of its second story, surmounted by a pigeon house. Père Merlier's sole vanity was to have this front plastered every ten years. It had just received a new coating and dazzled the village when the sun shone on it at noon.

For twenty years Père Merlier had been mayor of Rocreuse. He was esteemed for the fortune he had acquired. His wealth was estimated at something like eighty thousand francs, amassed sou by sou. When he married Madeleine Guillard, who brought him the mill as her dowry, he possessed only his two arms. But Madeleine never repented of her choice, so briskly did he manage the business. Now his wife was dead, and he remained a widower with his daughter Francoise. Certainly he might have rested, allowed the mill wheel to slumber in the moss, but that would have been too dull for him, and in his eyes the building would have seemed dead. He toiled on for pleasure.

Père Merlier was a tall old man with a long, still face, who never laughed but who possessed, notwithstanding, a very gay heart. He had been chosen mayor because of his money and also on account of the imposing air he could assume during a marriage ceremony.

Francoise Merlier was just eighteen. She did not pass for one of the handsome girls of the district, as she was not robust. Up to her fifteenth year she had been even ugly.

The Rocreuse people had not been able to understand why the daughter of Père and Mere Merlier, both of whom had always enjoyed excellent health, grew ill and with an air of regret. But at fifteen, though yet delicate, her little face became one of the prettiest in the world. She had black hair, black eyes, and was as rosy as a peach; her lips constantly wore a smile; there were dimples in her cheeks, and her fair forehead seemed crowned with sunlight. Although not considered robust in the district, she was far from thin; the idea was simply that she could not lift a sack of grain, but she would become plump as she grew older—she would eventually be as round and dainty as a quail. Her father's long periods of silence had made her thoughtful very young. If she smiled constantly it was to please others. By nature she was serious.

Of course all the young men of the district paid court to her, more on account of her ecus than her pretty ways. At last she made a choice which scandalized the community.

On the opposite bank of the Morelle lived a tall youth named Dominique Penquer. He did not belong to Rocreuse. Ten years before he had arrived from Belgium as the heir of his uncle, who had left him a small property upon the very border of the forest of Gagny, just opposite the mill, a few gunshots distant. He had come to sell this property, he said, and return home. But the district charmed him, it appeared, for he did not quit it. He was seen cultivating his little field, gathering a few vegetables upon which he subsisted. He fished and hunted; many times the forest guards nearly caught him and were on the point of drawing up procès-verbaux against him. This free existence, the resources of which the peasants could not clearly discover, at length gave him a bad reputation. He was vaguely styled a poacher. At any rate, he was lazy, for he was often found asleep on the grass when he should have been at work. The hut he inhabited beneath the last trees on the edge of the forest did not seem at all like the dwelling of an honest young fellow. If he had had dealings with the wolves of the ruins of Gagny the old women would not have been the least bit surprised. Nevertheless, the young girls sometimes risked defending him, for this doubtful man was superb; supple and tall as a poplar, he had a very white skin, with flaxen hair and beard which gleamed like gold in the sun.

One fine morning Francoise declared to Père Merlier that she loved Dominique and would never wed any other man.

It may well be imagined what a blow this was to Père Merlier. He said nothing, according to his custom, but his face grew thoughtful and his internal gaiety no longer sparkled in his eyes. He looked gruff for a week. Francoise also was exceedingly grave. What tormented Père Merlier was to find out how this rogue of a poacher had managed to fascinate his daughter. Dominique had never visited the mill. The miller watched and saw the gallant on the other side of the Morelle, stretched out upon the grass and feigning to be asleep. Francoise could see him from her chamber window. Everything was plain: they had fallen in love by casting sheep's eyes at each other over the mill wheel.

Another week went by. Francoise became more and more grave. Père Merlier still said nothing. Then one evening he himself silently brought in Dominique. Francoise at that moment was setting the table. She did not seem astonished; she contented herself with putting on an additional plate, knife and fork, but the little dimples were again seen in her cheeks, and her smile reappeared. That morning Père Merlier had sought out Dominique in his hut on the border of the wood.

There the two men had talked for three hours with doors and windows closed. What was the purport of their conversation no one ever knew. Certain it was, however, that Père Merlier, on taking his departure, already called Dominique his son-in-law. Without doubt the old man had found the youth he had gone to seek a worthy youth in the lazy fellow who stretched himself out upon the grass to make the girls fall in love with him.

All Rocreuse clamored. The women at the doors had plenty to say on the subject of the folly of Père Merlier, who had thus introduced a reprobate into his house. The miller let people talk on. Perhaps he remembered his own marriage. He was without a sou when he wedded Madeleine and her mill; this, however, had not prevented him from making a good husband. Besides, Dominique cut short the gossip by going so vigorously to work that all the district was amazed. The miller's assistant had just been drawn to serve as a soldier, and Dominique would not suffer another to be engaged. He carried the sacks, drove the cart, fought with the old mill wheel when it refused to turn, and all this with such good will that people came to see him out of curiosity. Père Merlier had his silent laugh. He was excessively proud of having formed a correct estimate of this youth. There is nothing like love to give courage to young folks. Amid all these heavy labors Francoise and Dominique adored each other. They did not indulge in lovers' talks, but there was a smiling gentleness in their glances.

Up to that time Père Merlier had not spoken a single word on the subject of marriage, and they respected this silence, awaiting the old man's will. Finally one day toward the middle of July he caused three tables to be placed in the courtyard, beneath the great elm, and invited his friends of Rocreuse to come in the evening and drink a glass of wine with him.

When the courtyard was full and all had their glasses in their hands, Père Merlier raised his very high and said:

"I have the pleasure to announce to you that Francoise will wed this young fellow here in a month, on Saint Louis's Day."

Then they drank noisily. Everybody smiled. But Père Merlier, again lifting his voice, exclaimed:

"Dominique, embrace your fiancee. It is your right."

They embraced, blushing to the tips of their ears, while all the guests laughed joyously. It was a genuine fête. They emptied a small cask of wine. Then when all were gone but intimate friends the conversation was carried on without noise. The night had fallen, a starry and cloudless night. Dominique and Francoise, seated side by side on a bench, said nothing.

An old peasant spoke of the war the emperor had declared against Prussia. All the village lads had already departed. On the preceding day troops had again passed through the place. There was going to be hard fighting.

"Bah!" said Père Merlier with the selfishness of a happy man. "Dominique is a foreigner; he will not go to the war. And if the Prussians come here he will be on hand to defend his wife!"

The idea that the Prussians might come there seemed a good joke. They were going to receive a sound whipping, and the affair would soon be over.

"I have afready seen them; I have already seen them," repeated the old peasant in a hollow voice.

There was silence. Then they drank again. Francoise and Dominique had heard nothing; they had gently taken each other by the hand behind the bench, so that nobody could see them, and it seemed so delightful that they remained where they were, their eyes plunged into the depths of the shadows.

What a warm and superb night it was! The village slumbered on both edges of the white highway in infantile quietude. From time to time was heard the crowing of some chanticleer aroused too soon. From the huge wood near by came long breaths, which passed over the roofs like caresses. The meadows, with their dark shadows, assumed a mysterious and dreamy majesty, while all the springs, all the flowing waters which gurgled in the darkness, seemed to be the cool and rhythmical respiration of the sleeping country. Occasionally the ancient mill wheel, lost in a doze, appeared to dream like those old watchdogs that bark while snoring; it cracked; it talked to itself, rocked by the fall of the Morelle, the surface of which gave forth the musical and continuous sound of an organ pipe. Never had more profound peace descended upon a happier corner of nature.

CHAPTER II
THE ATTACK ON THE MILL

A month later, on the day preceding that of Saint Louis, Rocreuse was in a state of terror. The Prussians had beaten the emperor and were advancing by forced marches toward the village. For a week past people who hurried along the highway had been announcing them thus: "They are at Lormiere—they are at Novelles!" And on hearing that they were drawing near so rapidly, Rocreuse every morning expected to see them descend from the wood of Gagny. They did not come, however, and that increased the fright. They would surely fall upon the village during the night and slaughter everybody.

That morning, a little before sunrise, there was an alarm. The inhabitants were awakened by the loud tramp of men on the highway. The women were already on their knees, making the sign of the cross, when some of the people, peering cautiously through the partially opened windows, recognized the red pantaloons. It was a French detachment. The captain immediately asked for the mayor of the district and remained at the mill after having talked with Père Merlier.

The sun rose gaily that morning. It would be hot at noon. Over the wood floated a golden brightness, while in the distance white vapors arose from the meadows. The neat and pretty village awoke amid the fresh air, and the country, with its river and its springs, had the moist sweetness of a bouquet. But that beautiful day caused nobody to smile. The captain was seen to take a turn around the mill, examine the neighboring houses, pass to the other side of the Morelle and from there study the district with a field glass; Père Merlier, who accompanied him, seemed to be giving him explanations. Then the captain posted soldiers behind the walls, behind the trees and in the ditches. The main body of the detachment encamped in the courtyard of the mill. Was there going to be a battle? When Père Merlier returned he was questioned. He nodded his head without speaking. Yes, there was going to be a battle!

Francoise and Dominique were in the courtyard; they looked at him. At last he took his pipe from his mouth and said:

"Ah, my poor young ones, you cannot get married tomorrow!"

Dominique, his lips pressed together, with an angry frown on his forehead, at times raised himself on tiptoe and fixed his eyes upon the wood of Gagny, as if he wished to see the Prussians arrive. Francoise, very pale and serious, came and went, furnishing the soldiers with what they needed. The troops were making soup in a corner of the courtyard; they joked while waiting for it to get ready.

The captain was delighted. He had visited the chambers and the huge hall of the mill which looked out upon the river. Now, seated beside the well, he was conversing with Père Merlier.

"Your mill is a real fortress," he said. "We can hold it without difficulty until evening. The bandits are late. They ought to be here."

The miller was grave. He saw his mill burning like a torch, but he uttered no complaint, thinking such a course useless. He merely said:

"You had better hide the boat behind the wheel; there is a place there just fit for that purpose. Perhaps it will be useful to have the boat."

The captain gave the requisite order. This officer was a handsome man of forty; he was tall and had an amiable countenance. The sight of Francoise and Dominique seemed to please him. He contemplated them as if he had forgotten the coming struggle. He followed Francoise with his eyes, and his look told plainly that he thought her charming. Then turning toward Dominique, he asked suddenly:

"Why are you not in the army, my good fellow?"

"I am a foreigner," answered the young man.

The captain evidently did not attach much weight to this reason. He winked his eye and smiled. Francoise was more agreeable company than a cannon. On seeing him smile, Dominique added:

"I am a foreigner, but I can put a ball in an apple at five hundred meters. There is my hunting gun behind you."

"You may have use for it," responded the captain dryly.

Francoise had approached, somewhat agitated. Without heeding the strangers present Dominique took and grasped in his the two hands she extended to him, as if to put herself under his protection. The captain smiled again but said not a word. He remained seated, his sword across his knees and his eyes plunged into space, lost in a reverie.

It was already ten o'clock. The heat had become very great. A heavy silence prevailed. In the courtyard, in the shadows of the sheds, the soldiers had begun to eat their soup. Not a sound came from the village; all its inhabitants had barricaded the doors and windows of their houses. A dog, alone upon the highway, howled. From the neighboring forests and meadows, swooning in the heat, came a prolonged and distant voice made up of all the scattered breaths. A cuckoo sang. Then the silence grew more intense.

Suddenly in that slumbering air a shot was heard. The captain leaped briskly to his feet; the soldiers left their plates of soup, yet half full. In a few seconds everybody was at the post of duty; from bottom to top the mill was occupied. Meanwhile the captain, who had gone out upon the road, had discovered nothing; to the right and to the left the highway stretched out, empty and white. A second shot was heard, and still nothing visible, not even a shadow. But as he was returning the captain perceived in the direction of Gagny, between two trees, a light puff of smoke whirling away like thistledown. The wood was calm and peaceful.

"The bandits have thrown themselves into the forest," he muttered. "They know we are here."

Then the firing continued, growing more and more vigorous, between the French soldiers posted around the mill and the Prussians hidden behind the trees. The balls whistled above the Morelle without damaging either side. The fusillade was irregular, the shots coming from every bush, and still only the little puffs of smoke, tossed gently by the breeze, were seen. This lasted nearly two hours. The officer hummed a tune with an air of indifference. Francoise and Dominique, who had remained in the courtyard, raised themselves on tiptoe and looked over a low wall. They were particularly interested in a little soldier posted on the shore of the Morelle, behind the remains of an old bateau; he stretched himself out flat on the ground, watched, fired and then glided into a ditch a trifle farther back to reload his gun; and his movements were so droll, so tricky and so supple, that they smiled as they looked at him. He must have perceived the head of a Prussian, for he arose quickly and brought his weapon to his shoulder, but before he could fire he uttered a cry, fell and rolled into the ditch, where for an instant his legs twitched convulsively like the claws of a chicken just killed. The little soldier had received a ball full in the breast. He was the first man slain. Instinctively Francoise seized Dominique's hand and clasped it with a nervous contraction.

"Move away," said the captain. "You are within range of the balls."

At that moment a sharp little thud was heard in the old elm, and a fragment of a branch came whirling down. But the two young folks did not stir; they were nailed to the spot by anxiety to see what was going on. On the edge of the wood a Prussian had suddenly come out from behind a tree as from a theater stage entrance, beating the air with his hands and falling backward. Nothing further moved; the two corpses seemed asleep in the broad sunlight; not a living soul was seen in the scorching country. Even the crack of the fusillade had ceased. The Morelle alone whispered in its clear tones.

Père Merlier looked at the captain with an air of surprise, as if to ask him if the struggle was over.

"They are getting ready for something worse," muttered the officer. "Don't trust appearances. Move away from there."

He had not finished speaking when there was a terrible discharge of musketry. The great elm was riddled, and a host of leaves shot into the air. The Prussians had happily fired too high. Dominique dragged, almost carried, Francoise away, while Père Merlier followed them, shouting:

"Go down into the cellar; the walls are solid!"

But they did not heed him; they entered the huge hall where ten soldiers were waiting in silence, watching through the chinks in the closed window shutters. The captain was alone in the courtyard, crouching behind the little wall, while the furious discharges continued. Without, the soldiers he had posted gave ground only foot by foot. However, they re-entered one by one, crawling, when the enemy had dislodged them from their hiding places. Their orders were to gain time and not show themselves, that the Prussians might remain in ignorance as to what force was before them. Another hour went by. As a sergeant arrived, saying that but two or three more men remained without, the captain glanced at his watch, muttering:

"Half-past two o'clock. We must hold the position four hours longer."

He caused the great gate of the courtyard to be closed, and every preparation was made for an energetic resistance. As the Prussians were on the opposite side of the Morelle, an immediate assault was not to be feared. There was a bridge two kilometers away, but they evidently were not aware of its existence, and it was hardly likely that they would attempt to ford the river. The officer, therefore, simply ordered the highway to be watched. Every effort would be made in the direction of the country.

Again the fusillade had ceased. The mill seemed dead beneath the glowing sun. Not a shutter was open; no sound came from the interior. At length, little by little, the Prussians showed themselves at the edge of the forest of Gagny. They stretched their necks and grew bold. In the mill several soldiers had already raised their guns to their shoulders, but the captain cried:

"No, no; wait. Let them come nearer."

They were exceedingly prudent, gazing at the mill with a suspicious air. The silent and somber old structure with its curtains of ivy filled them with uneasiness. Nevertheless, they advanced. When fifty of them were in the opposite meadow the officer uttered the single word:

"Fire!"

A crash was heard; isolated shots followed. Francoise, all of a tremble, had mechanically put her hands to her ears. Dominique, behind the soldiers, looked on; when the smoke had somewhat lifted he saw three Prussians stretched upon their backs in the center of the meadow. The others had thrown themselves behind the willows and poplars. Then the siege began.

For more than an hour the mill was riddled with balls. They dashed against the old walls like hail. When they struck the stones they were heard to flatten and fall into the water. They buried themselves in the wood with a hollow sound. Occasionally a sharp crack announced that the mill wheel had been hit. The soldiers in the interior were careful of their shots; they fired only when they could take aim. From time to time the captain consulted his watch. As a ball broke a shutter and plowed into the ceiling he said to himself:

"Four o'clock. We shall never be able to hold out!"

Little by little the terrible fusillade weakened the old mill. A shutter fell into the water, pierced like a bit of lace, and it was necessary to replace it with a mattress. Père Merlier constantly exposed himself to ascertain the extent of the damage done to his poor wheel, the cracking of which made his heart ache. All would be over with it this time; never could he repair it. Dominique had implored Francoise to withdraw, but she refused to leave him; she was seated behind a huge oaken clothespress, which protected her. A ball, however, struck the clothespress, the sides of which gave forth a hollow sound. Then Dominique placed himself in front of Francoise. He had not yet fired a shot; he held his gun in his hand but was unable to approach the windows, which were altogether occupied by the soldiers. At each discharge the floor shook.

"Attention! Attention!" suddenly cried the captain.

He had just seen a great dark mass emerge from the wood. Immediately a formidable platoon fire opened. It was like a waterspout passing over the mill. Another shutter was shattered, and through the gaping opening of the window the balls entered. Two soldiers rolled upon the floor. One of them lay like a stone; they pushed the body against the wall because it was in the way. The other twisted in agony, begging his comrades to finish him, but they paid no attention to him. The balls entered in a constant stream; each man took care of himself and strove to find a loophole through which to return the fire. A third soldier was hit; he uttered not a word; he fell on the edge of a table, with eyes fixed and haggard. Opposite these dead men Francoise, stricken with horror, had mechanically pushed away her chair to sit on the floor against the wall; she thought she would take up less room there and not be in so much danger. Meanwhile the soldiers had collected all the mattresses of the household and partially stopped up the windows with them. The hall was filled with wrecks, with broken weapons and demolished furniture.

"Five o'clock," said the captain. "Keep up your courage! They are about to try to cross the river!"

At that moment Francoise uttered a cry. A ball which had ricocheted had grazed her forehead. Several drops of blood appeared. Dominique stared at her; then, approaching the window, he fired his first shot. Once started, he did not stop. He loaded and fired without heeding what was passing around him, but from time to time he glanced at Francoise. He was very deliberate and aimed with care. The Prussians, keeping beside the poplars, attempted the passage of the Morelle, as the captain had predicted, but as soon as a man strove to cross he fell, shot in the head by Dominique. The captain, who had his eyes on the young man, was amazed. He complimented him, saying that he should be glad to have many such skillful marksmen. Dominique did not hear him. A ball cut his shoulder; another wounded his arm, but he continued to fire.

There were two more dead men. The mangled mattresses no longer stopped the windows. The last discharge seemed as if it would have carried away the mill. The position had ceased to be tenable. Nevertheless, the captain said firmly:

"Hold your ground for half an hour more!"

Now he counted the minutes. He had promised his chiefs to hold the enemy in check there until evening, and he would not give an inch before the hour he had fixed on for the retreat. He preserved his amiable air and smiled upon Francoise to reassure her. He had picked up the gun of a dead soldier and himself was firing.

Only four soldiers remained in the hall. The Prussians appeared in a body on the other side of the Morelle, and it was clear that they intended speedily to cross the river. A few minutes more elapsed. The stubborn captain would not order the retreat. Just then a sergeant hastened to him and said:

"They are upon the highway; they will take us in the rear!"

The Prussians must have found the bridge. The captain pulled out his watch and looked at it.

"Five minutes longer," he said. "They cannot get here before that time!"

Then at six o'clock exactly he at last consented to lead his men out through a little door which opened into a lane. From there they threw themselves into a ditch; they gained the forest of Sauval. Before taking his departure the captain bowed very politely to Père Merlier and made his excuses, adding:

"Amuse them! We will return!"

Dominique was now alone in the hall. He was still firing, hearing nothing, understanding nothing. He felt only the need of defending Francoise. He had not the least suspicion in the world that the soldiers had retreated. He aimed and killed his man at every shot. Suddenly there was a loud noise. The Prussians had entered the courtyard from behind. Dominique fired a last; shot, and they fell upon him while his gun was yet smoking.

Four men held him. Others vociferated around him in a frightful language. They were ready to slaughter him on the spot. Francoise, with a supplicating look, had cast herself before him. But an officer entered and ordered the prisoner to be delivered up to him. After exchanging a few words in German with the soldiers he turned toward Dominique and said to him roughly in very good French:

"You will be shot in two hours!"

CHAPTER III
THE FLIGHT

It was a settled rule of the German staff that every Frenchman, not belonging to the regular army, taken with arms in his hands should be shot. The militia companies themselves were not recognized as belligerents. By thus making terrible examples of the peasants who defended their homes, the Germans hoped to prevent the levy en masse, which they feared.

The officer, a tall, lean man of fifty, briefly questioned Dominique. Although he spoke remarkably pure French he had a stiffness altogether Prussian.

"Do you belong to this district?" he asked.

"No; I am a Belgian," answered the young man.

"Why then did you take up arms? The fighting did not concern you!"

Dominique made no reply. At that moment the officer saw Francoise who was standing by, very pale, listening; upon her white forehead her slight wound had put a red bar. He looked at the young folks, one after the other, seemed to understand matters and contented himself with adding:

"You do not deny having fired, do you?"

"I fired as often as I could!" responded Dominique tranquilly.

This confession was useless, for he was black with powder, covered with sweat and stained with a few drops of blood which had flowed from the scratch on his shoulder.

"Very well," said the officer. "You will be shot in two hours!"

Francoise did not cry out. She clasped her hands and raised them with a gesture of mute despair. The officer noticed this gesture. Two soldiers had taken Dominique to a neighboring apartment, where they were to keep watch over him. The young girl had fallen upon a chair, totally overcome; she could not weep; she was suffocating. The officer had continued to examine her. At last he spoke to her.

"Is that young man your brother?" he demanded.

She shook her head negatively. The German stood stiffly on his feet with out a smile. Then after a short silence he again asked:

"Has he lived long in the district?"

She nodded affirmatively.

"In that case, he ought to be thoroughly acquainted with the neighboring forests."

This time she spoke.

"He is thoroughly acquainted with them, monsieur," she said, looking at him with considerable surprise.

He said nothing further to her but turned upon his heel, demanding that the mayor of the village should be brought to him. But Francoise had arisen with a slight blush on her countenance; thinking that she had seized the aim of the officer's questions, she had recovered hope. She herself ran to find her father.

Père Merlier, as soon as the firing had ceased, had quickly descended to the wooden gallery to examine his wheel. He adored his daughter; he had a solid friendship for Dominique, his future son-in-law, but his wheel also held a large place in his heart. Since the two young ones, as he called them, had come safe and sound out of the fight, he thought of his other tenderness, which had suffered greatly. Bent over the huge wooden carcass, he was studying its wounds with a sad air. Five buckets were shattered to pieces; the central framework was riddled. He thrust his fingers in the bullet holes to measure their depth; he thought how he could repair all these injuries. Francoise found him already stopping up the clefts with rubbish and moss.

"Father," she said, "you are wanted."

And she wept at last as she told him what she had just heard. Père Merlier tossed his head. People were not shot in such a summary fashion. The matter must be looked after. He re-entered the mill with his silent and tranquil air. When the officer demanded of him provisions for his men he replied that the inhabitants of Rocreuse were not accustomed to be treated roughly and that nothing would be obtained from them if violence were employed. He would see to everything but on condition that he was not interfered with. The officer at first seemed irritated by his calm tone; then he gave way before the old man's short and clear words. He even called him back and asked him:

"What is the name of that wood opposite?"

"The forest of Sauval."

"What is its extent?"

The miller looked at him fixedly.

"I do not know," he answered.

And he went away. An hour later the contribution of war in provisions and money, demanded by the officer, was in the courtyard of the mill. Night came on. Francoise watched with anxiety the movements of the soldiers. She hung about the room in which Dominique was imprisoned. Toward seven o'clock she experienced a poignant emotion. She saw the officer enter the prisoner's apartment and for a quarter of an hour heard their voices in loud conversation. For an instant the officer reappeared upon the threshold to give an order in German, which she did not understand, but when twelve men ranged themselves in the courtyard, their guns on their shoulders, she trembled and felt as if about to faint. All then was over: the execution was going to take place. The twelve men stood there ten minutes, Dominique's voice continuing to be raised in a tone of violent refusal. Finally the officer came out, saying, as he roughly shut the door:

"Very well; reflect. I give you until tomorrow morning."

And with a gesture he ordered the twelve men to break ranks. Francoise was stupefied. Père Merlier, who had been smoking his pipe and looking at the platoon simply with an air of curiosity, took her by the arm with paternal gentleness. He led her to her chamber.

"Be calm," he said, "and try to sleep. Tomorrow, when it is light, we will see what can be done."

As he withdrew he prudently locked her in. It was his opinion that women were good for nothing and that they spoiled everything when they took a hand in a serious affair. But Francoise did not retire. She sat for a long while upon the side of her bed, listening to the noises of the house. The German soldiers encamped in the courtyard sang and laughed; they must have been eating and drinking until eleven o'clock, for the racket did not cease an instant. In the mill itself heavy footsteps resounded from time to time, without doubt those of the sentinels who were being relieved. But she was interested most by the sounds she could distinguish in the apartment beneath her chamber. Many times she stretched herself out at full length and put her ear to the floor. That apartment was the one in which Dominique was confined. He must have been walking back and forth from the window to the wall, for she long heard the regular cadence of his steps. Then deep silence ensued; he had doubtless seated himself. Finally every noise ceased and all was as if asleep. When slumber appeared to her to have settled on the house she opened her window as gently as possible and leaned her elbows on the sill.

Without, the night had a warm serenity. The slender crescent of the moon, which was sinking behind the forest of Sauval, lit up the country with the glimmer of a night lamp. The lengthened shadows of the tall trees barred the meadows with black, while the grass in uncovered spots assumed the softness of greenish velvet. But Francoise did not pause to admire the mysterious charms of the night. She examined the country, searching for the sentinels whom the Germans had posted obliquely. She clearly saw their shadows extending like the rounds of a ladder along the Morelle. Only one was before the mill, on the other shore of the river, beside a willow, the branches of which dipped in the water. Francoise saw him plainly. He was a tall man and was standing motionless, his face turned toward the sky with the dreamy air of a shepherd.

When she had carefully inspected the locality she again seated herself on her bed. She remained there an hour, deeply absorbed. Then she listened once more: there was not a sound in the mill. She returned to the window and glanced out, but doubtless one of the horns of the moon, which was still visible behind the trees, made her uneasy, for she resumed her waiting attitude. At last she thought the proper time had come. The night was as black as jet; she could no longer see the sentinel opposite; the country spread out like a pool of ink. She strained her ear for an instant and made her decision. Passing near the window was an iron ladder, the bars fastened to the wall, which mounted from the wheel to the garret and formerly enabled the millers to reach certain machinery; afterward the mechanism had been altered, and for a long while the ladder had been hidden under the thick ivy which covered that side of the mill.

Francoise bravely climbed out of her window and grasped one of the bars of the ladder. She began to descend. Her skirts embarrassed her greatly. Suddenly a stone was detached from the wall and fell into the Morelle with a loud splash. She stopped with an icy shiver of fear. Then she realized that the waterfall with its continuous roar would drown every noise she might make, and she descended more courageously, feeling the ivy with her foot, assuring herself that the rounds were firm. When she was at the height of the chamber which served as Dominique's prison she paused. An unforeseen difficulty nearly caused her to lose all her courage: the window of the chamber was not directly below that of her apartment. She hung off from the ladder, but when she stretched out her arm her hand encountered only the wall. Must she, then, ascend without pushing her plan to completion? Her arms were fatigued; the murmur of the Morelle beneath her commenced to make her dizzy. Then she tore from the wall little fragments of plaster and threw them against Dominique's window. He did not hear; he was doubtless asleep. She crumbled more plaster from the wall, scraping the skin off her fingers. She was utterly exhausted; she felt herself falling backward, when Dominique at last softly opened the window.

"It is I!" she murmured. "Catch me quickly; I'm falling!"

It was the first time that she had addressed him familiarly. Leaning out, he seized her and drew her into the chamber. There she gave vent to a flood of tears, stifling her sobs that she might not be heard. Then by a supreme effort she calmed herself.

"Are you guarded?" she asked in a low voice.

Dominique, still stupefied at seeing her thus, nodded his head affirmatively, pointing to the door. On the other side they heard someone snoring; the sentinel, yielding to sleep, had thrown himself on the floor against the door, arguing that by disposing himself thus the prisoner could not escape.

"You must fly," resumed Francoise excitedly. "I have come to beg you to do so and to bid you farewell."

But he did not seem to hear her. He repeated:

"What? Is it you; is it you? Oh, what fear you caused me! You might have killed yourself!"

He seized her hands; he kissed them.

"How I love you, Francoise!" he murmured. "You are as courageous as good. I had only one dread: that I should die without seeing you again. But you are here, and now they can shoot me. When I have passed a quarter of an hour with you I shall be ready."

Little by little he had drawn her to him, and she leaned her head upon his shoulder. The danger made them dearer to each other. They forgot everything in that warm clasp.

"Ah, Francoise," resumed Dominique in a caressing voice, "this is Saint Louis's Day, the day, so long awaited, of our marriage. Nothing has been able to separate us, since we are both here alone, faithful to the appointment. Is not this our wedding morning?"

"Yes, yes," she repeated, "it is our wedding morning."

They tremblingly exchanged a kiss. But all at once she disengaged herself from Dominique's arms; she remembered the terrible reality.

"You must fly; you must fly," she whispered. "There is not a minute to be lost!"

And as he stretched out his arms in the darkness to clasp her again, she said tenderly:

"Oh, I implore you to listen to me! If you die I shall die also! In an hour it will be light. I want you to go at once."

Then rapidly she explained her plan. The iron ladder descended to the mill wheel; there he could climb down the buckets and get into the boat which was hidden away in a nook. Afterward it would be easy for him to reach the other bank of the river and escape.

"But what of the sentinels?" he asked.

"There is only one, opposite, at the foot of the first willow."

"What if he should see me and attempt to give an alarm?"

Francoise shivered. She placed in his hand a knife she had brought with her. There was a brief silence.

"What is to become of your father and yourself?" resumed Dominique. "No, I cannot fly! When I am gone those soldiers will, perhaps, massacre you both! You do not know them. They offered me my life if I would consent to guide them through the forest of Sauval. When they discover my escape they will be capable of anything!"

The young girl did not stop to argue. She said simply in reply to all the reasons he advanced:

"Out of love for me, fly! If you love me, Dominique, do not remain here another moment!"

Then she promised to climb back to her chamber. No one would know that she had helped him. She finally threw her arms around him to convince him with an embrace, with a burst of extraordinary love. He was vanquished. He asked but one more question:

"Can you swear to me that your father knows what you have done and that he advises me to fly?"

"My father sent me!" answered Francoise boldly.

She told a falsehood. At that moment she had only one immense need: to know that he was safe, to escape from the abominable thought that the sun would be the signal for his death. When he was far away every misfortune might fall upon her; that would seem delightful to her from the moment he was secure. The selfishness of her tenderness desired that he should live before everything.

"Very well," said Dominique; "I will do what you wish."

They said nothing more. Dominique reopened the window. But suddenly a sound froze them. The door was shaken, and they thought that it was about to be opened. Evidently a patrol had heard their voices. Standing locked in each other's arms, they waited in unspeakable anguish. The door was shaken a second time, but it did not open. They uttered low sighs of relief; they comprehended that the soldier who was asleep against the door must have turned over. In fact, silence succeeded; the snoring was resumed.

Dominique exacted that Francoise should ascend to her chamber before he departed. He clasped her in his arms and bade her a mute adieu. Then he aided her to seize the ladder and clung to it in his turn. But he refused to descend a single round until convinced that she was in her apartment. When Francoise had entered her window she let fall in a voice as light as a breath:

"Au revoir, my love!"

She leaned her elbows on the sill and strove to follow Dominique with her eyes. The night was yet very dark. She searched for the sentinel but could not see him; the willow alone made a pale stain in the midst of the gloom. For an instant she heard the sound produced by Dominique's body in passing along the ivy. Then the wheel cracked, and there was a slight agitation in the water which told her that the young man had found the boat. A moment afterward she distinguished the somber silhouette of the bateau on the gray surface of the Morelle. Terrible anguish seized upon her. Each instant she thought she heard the sentinel's cry of alarm; the smallest sounds scattered through the gloom seemed to her the hurried tread of soldiers, the clatter of weapons, the charging of guns. Nevertheless, the seconds elapsed and the country maintained its profound peace. Dominique must have reached the other side of the river. Francoise saw nothing more. The silence was majestic. She heard a shuffling of feet, a hoarse cry and the hollow fall of a body. Afterward the silence grew deeper. Then as if she had felt Death pass by, she stood, chilled through and through, staring into the thick night.

CHAPTER IV
A TERRIBLE EXPERIENCE

At dawn a clamor of voices shook the mill. Père Merlier opened the door of Francoise's chamber. She went down into the courtyard, pale and very calm. But there she could not repress a shiver as she saw the corpse of a Prussian soldier stretched out on a cloak beside the well.

Around the body troops gesticulated, uttering cries of fury. Many of them shook their fists at the village. Meanwhile the officer had summoned Père Merlier as the mayor of the commune.

"Look!" he said to him in a voice almost choking with anger. "There lies one of our men who was found assassinated upon the bank of the river. We must make a terrible example, and I count on you to aid us in discovering the murderer."

"As you choose," answered the miller with his usual stoicism, "but you will find it no easy task."

The officer stooped and drew aside a part of the cloak which hid the face of the dead man. Then appeared a horrible wound. The sentinel had been struck in the throat, and the weapon had remained in the cut. It was a kitchen knife with a black handle.

"Examine that knife," said the officer to Père Merlier; "perhaps it will help us in our search."

The old man gave a start but recovered control of himself immediately. He replied without moving a muscle of his face:

"Everybody in the district has similar knives. Doubtless your man was weary of fighting and put an end to his own life. It looks like it!"

"Mind what you say!" cried the officer furiously. "I do not know what prevents me from setting fire to the four corners of the village!"

Happily in his rage he did not notice the deep trouble pictured on Francoise's countenance. She had been forced to sit down on a stone bench near the well. Despite herself her eyes were fixed upon the corpse stretched our on the ground almost at her feet. It was that of a tall and handsome man who resembled Dominique, with flaxen hair and blue eyes. This resemblance made her heart ache. She thought that perhaps the dead soldier had left behind him in Germany a sweetheart who would weep her eyes out for him. She recognized her knife in the throat of the murdered man. She had killed him.

The officer was talking of striking Rocreuse with terrible measures, when soldiers came running to him. Dominique's escape had just been discovered. It caused an extreme agitation. The officer went to the apartment in which the prisoner had been confined, looked out of the window which had remained open, understood everything and returned, exasperated.

Père Merlier seemed greatly vexed by Dominique's flight.

"The imbecile!" he muttered. "He has ruined all!"

Francoise heard him and was overcome with anguish. But the miller did not suspect her of complicity in the affair. He tossed his head, saying to her in an undertone:

"We are in a nice scrape!"

"It was that wretch who assassinated the soldier! I am sure of it!" cried the officer. "He has undoubtedly reached the forest. But he must be found for us or the village shall pay for him!"

Turning to the miller, he said:

"See here, you ought to know where he is hidden!"

Père Merlier laughed silently, pointing to the wide stretch of wooden hills.

"Do you expect to find a man in there?" he said.

"Oh, there must be nooks there with which you are acquainted. I will give you ten men. You must guide them."

"As you please. But it will take a week to search all the wood in the vicinity."

The old man's tranquillity enraged the officer. In fact, the latter comprehended the asburdity of this search. At that moment he saw Francoise, pale and trembling, on the bench. The anxious attitude of the young girl struck him. He was silent for an instant, during which he in turn examined the miller and his daughter.

At length he demanded roughly of the old man:

"Is not that fellow your child's lover?"

Père Merlier grew livid and seemed about to hurl himself upon the officer to strangle him. He stiffened himself but made no answer. Francoise buried her face in her hands.

"Yes, that's it!" continued the Prussian. "And you or your daughter helped him to escape! One of you is his accomplice! For the last time, will you give him up to us?"

The miller uttered not a word. He turned away and looked into space with an air of indifference, as if the officer had not addressed him. This brought the latter's rage to a head.

"Very well!" he shouted. "You shall be shot in his place!"

And he again ordered out the platoon of execution. Père Merlier remained as stoical as ever. He hardly even shrugged his shoulders; all this drama appeared to him in bad taste. Without doubt he did not believe that they would shoot a man so lightly. But when the platoon drew up before him he said gravely:

"So it is serious, is it? Go on with your bloody work then! If you must have a victim I will do as well as another!"

But Francoise started up, terrified, stammering:

"In pity, monsieur, do no harm to my father! Kill me in his stead! I aided Dominique to fly! I alone am guilty!"

"Hush, my child!" cried Père Merlier. "Why do you tell an untruth? She passed the night locked in her chamber, monsieur. She tells a falsehood, I assure you!"

"No, I do not tell a falsehood!" resumed the young girl ardently. "I climbed out of my window and went down the iron ladder; I urged Dominique to fly. This is the truth, the whole truth!"

The old man became very pale. He saw clearly in her eyes that she did not lie, and her story terrified him. Ah, these children with their hearts, how they spoil everything! Then he grew angry and exclaimed:

"She is mad; do not heed her. She tells you stupid tales. Come, finish your work!"

She still protested. She knelt, clasping her hands. The officer tranquilly watched this dolorous struggle.

"MON DIEU!" he said at last. "I take your father because I have not the other. Find the fugitive and the old man shall be set at liberty!"

She gazed at him with staring eyes, astonished at the atrocity of the proposition.

"How horrible!" she murmured. "Where do you think I can find Dominique at this hour? He has departed; I know no more about him."

"Come, make your choice—him or your father."

"Oh, MON DIEU! How can I choose? If I knew where Dominique was I could not choose! You are cutting my heart. I would rather die at once. Yes, it would be the sooner over. Kill me, I implore you, kill me!"

This scene of despair and tears finally made the officer impatient. He cried out:

"Enough! I will be merciful. I consent to give you two hours. If in that time your lover is not here your father will be shot in his place!"

He caused Père Merlier to be taken to the chamber which had served as Dominique's prison. The old man demanded tobacco and began to smoke. Upon his impassible face not the slightest emotion was visible. But when alone, as he smoked, he shed two big tears which ran slowly down his cheeks. His poor, dear child, how she was suffering!

Francoise remained in the middle of the courtyard. Prussian soldiers passed, laughing. Some of them spoke to her, uttered jokes she could not understand. She stared at the door through which her father had disappeared. With a slow movement she put her hand to her forehead, as if to prevent it from bursting.

The officer turned upon his heel, saying:

"You have two hours. Try to utilize them."

She had two hours. This phrase buzzed in her ears. Then mechanically she quitted the courtyard; she walked straight ahead. Where should she go?—what should she do? She did not even try to make a decision because she well understood the inutility of her efforts. However, she wished to see Dominique. They could have an understanding together; they might, perhaps, find an expedient. And amid the confusion of her thoughts she went down to the shore of the Morelle, which she crossed below the sluice at a spot where there were huge stones. Her feet led her beneath the first willow, in the corner of the meadow. As she stooped she saw a pool of blood which made her turn pale. It was there the murder had been committed. She followed the track of Dominique in the trodden grass; he must have run, for she perceived a line of long footprints stretching across the meadow. Then farther on she lost these traces. But in a neighboring field she thought she found them again. The new trail conducted her to the edge of the forest, where every indication was effaced.

Francoise, nevertheless, plunged beneath the trees. It solaced her to be alone. She sat down for an instant, but at the thought that time was passing she leaped to her feet. How long had it been since she left the mill? Five minutes?—half an hour? She had lost all conception of time. Perhaps Dominique had concealed himself in a copse she knew of, where they had one afternoon eaten filberts together. She hastened to the copse, searched it. Only a blackbird flew away, uttering its soft, sad note. Then she thought he might have taken refuge in a hollow of the rocks, where it had sometimes been his custom to lie in wait for game, but the hollow of the rocks was empty. What good was it to hunt for him? She would never find him, but little by little the desire to discover him took entire possession of her, and she hastened her steps. The idea that he might have climbed a tree suddenly occurred to her. She advanced with uplifted eyes, and that he might be made aware of her presence she called him every fifteen or twenty steps. Cuckoos answered; a breath of wind which passed through the branches made her believe that he was there and was descending. Once she even imagined she saw him; she stopped, almost choked, and wished to fly. What was she to say to him? Had she come to take him back to be shot? Oh no, she would not tell him what had happened. She would cry out to him to escape, not to remain in the neighborhood. Then the thought that her father was waiting for her gave her a sharp pain. She fell upon the turf, weeping, crying aloud:

"MON DIEU! MON DIEU! Why am I here?"

She was mad to have come. And as if seized with fear, she ran; she sought to leave the forest. Three times she deceived herself; she thought she never again would find the mill, when she entered a meadow just opposite Rocreuse. As soon as she saw the village she paused. Was she going to return alone? She was still hesitating when a voice softly called:

"Francoise! Francoise!"

And she saw Dominique, who had raised his head above the edge of a ditch. Just God! She had found him! Did heaven wish his death? She restrained a cry; she let herself glide into the ditch.

"Are you searching for me?" asked the young man.

"Yes," she answered, her brain in a whirl, not knowing what she said.

"What has happened?"

She lowered her eyes, stammered:

"Nothing. I was uneasy; I wanted to see you."

Then, reassured, he explained to her that he had resolved not to g away. He was doubtful about the safety of herself and her father. Thos

Prussian wretches were fully capable of taking vengeance upon women and old men. But everything was getting on well. He added with a laugh:

"Our wedding will take place in a week—I am sure of it."

Then as she remained overwhelmed, he grew grave again and said:

"But what ails you? You are concealing something from me!"

"No; I swear it to you. I am out of breath from running."

He embraced her, saying that it was imprudent for them to be talking, and he wished to climb out of the ditch to return to the forest. She restrained him. She trembled.

"Listen," she said: "it would, perhaps, be wise for you to remain where you are. No one is searching for you; you have nothing to fear."

"Francoise, you are concealing something from me," he repeated.

Again she swore that she was hiding nothing. She had simply wished to know that he was near her. And she stammered forth still further reasons. She seemed so strange to him that he now could not be induced to flee. Besides, he had faith in the return of the French. Troops had been seen in the direction of Sauval.

"Ah, let them hurry; let them get here as soon as possible," she murmured fervently.

At that moment eleven o'clock sounded from the belfry of Rocreuse. The strokes were clear and distinct. She arose with a terrified look; two hours had passed since she quitted the mill.

"Hear me," she said rapidly: "if we have need of you I will wave my handkerchief from my chamber window."

And she departed on a run, while Dominique, very uneasy, stretched himself out upon the edge of the ditch to watch the mill. As she was about to enter Rocreuse, Francoise met an old beggar, Père Bontemps, who knew everybody in the district. He bowed to her; he had just seen the miller in the midst of the Prussians; then, making the sign of the cross and muttering broken words, he went on his way.

"The two hours have passed," said the officer when Francoise appeared.

Père Merlier was there, seated upon the bench beside the well. He was smoking. The young girl again begged, wept, sank on her knees. She wished to gain time. The hope of seeing the French return had increased in her, and while lamenting she thought she heard in the distance, the measured tramp of an army. Oh, if they would come, if they would deliver them all?

"Listen, monsieur," she said: "an hour, another hour; you can grant us another hour!"

But the officer remained inflexible. He even ordered two men to seize her and take her away, that they might quietly proceed with the execution of the old man. Then a frightful struggle took place in Francoise's heart. She could not allow her father to be thus assassinated. No, no; she would die rather with Dominique. She was running toward her chamber when Dominique himself entered the courtyard.

The officer and the soldiers uttered a shout of triumph. But the young man, calmly, with a somewhat severe look, went up to Francoise, as if she had been the only person present.

"You did wrong," he said. "Why did you not bring me back? It remained for Père Bontemps to tell me everything. But I am here!"

CHAPTER V
THE RETURN OF THE FRENCH

It was three o'clock in the afternoon. Great black clouds, the trail of some neighboring storm, had slowly filled the sky. The yellow heavens, the brass covered uniforms, had changed the valley of Rocreuse, so gay in the sunlight, into a den of cutthroats full of sinister gloom. The Prussian officer had contented himself with causing Dominique to be imprisoned without announcing what fate he reserved for him. Since noon Francoise had been torn by terrible anguish. Despite her father's entreaties she would not quit the courtyard. She was awaiting the French. But the hours sped on; night was approaching, and she suffered the more as all the time gained did not seem to be likely to change the frightful denouement.

About three o'clock the Prussians made their preparations for departure. For an instant past the officer had, as on the previous day, shut himself up with Dominique. Francoise realized that the young man's life was in balance. She clasped her hands; she prayed. Père Merlier, beside her, maintained silence and the rigid attitude of an old peasant who does not struggle against fate.

"Oh, MON DIEU! Oh, MON DIEU!" murmured Francoise. "They are going to kill him!"

The miller drew her to him and took her on his knees as if she had been a child.

At that moment the officer came out, while behind him two men brought Dominique.

"Never! Never!" cried the latter. "I am ready to die!"

"Think well," resumed the officer. "The service you refuse me another will render us. I am generous: I offer you your life. I want you simply to guide us through the forest to Montredon. There must be pathways leading there."

Dominique was silent.

"So you persist in your infatuation, do you?"

"Kill me and end all this!" replied the young man.

Francoise, her hands clasped, supplicated him from afar. She had forgotten everything; she would have advised him to commit an act of cowardice. But Père Merlier seized her hands that the Prussians might not see her wild gestures.

"He is right," he whispered: "it is better to die!"

The platoon of execution was there. The officer awaited a sign of weakness on Dominique's part. He still expected to conquer him. No one spoke. In the distance violent crashes of thunder were heard. Oppressive heat weighed upon the country. But suddenly, amid the silence, a cry broke forth:

"The French! The French!"

Yes, the French were at hand. Upon the Sauval highway, at the edge of the wood, the line of red pantaloons could be distinguished. In the mill there was an extraordinary agitation. The Prussian soldiers ran hither and thither with guttural exclamations. Not a shot had yet been fired.

"The French! The French!" cried Francoise, clapping her hands.

She was wild with joy. She escaped from her father's grasp; she laughed and tossed her arms in the air. At last they had come and come in time, since Dominique was still alive!

A terrible platoon fire, which burst upon her ears like a clap of thunder, caused her to turn. The officer muttered between his teeth:

"Before everything, let us settle this affair!"

And with his own hand pushing Dominique against the wall of a shed he ordered his men to fire. When Francoise looked Dominique lay upon the ground with blood streaming from his neck and shoulders.

She did not weep; she stood stupefied. Her eyes grew fixed, and she sat down under the shed, a few paces from the body. She stared at it, wringing her hands. The Prussians had seized Père Merlier as a hostage.

It was a stirring combat. The officer had rapidly posted his men, comprehending that he could not beat a retreat without being cut to pieces. Hence he would fight to the last. Now the Prussians defended the mill, and the French attacked it. The fusillade began with unusual violence. For half an hour it did not cease. Then a hollow sound was heard, and a ball broke a main branch of the old elm. The French had cannon. A battery, stationed just above the ditch in which Dominique had hidden himself, swept the wide street of Rocreuse. The struggle could not last long.

Ah, the poor mill! Balls pierced it in every part. Half of the roof was carried away. Two walls were battered down. But it was on the side of the Morelle that the destruction was most lamentable. The ivy, torn from the tottering edifice, hung like rags; the river was encumbered with wrecks of all kinds, and through a breach was visible Francoise's chamber with its bed, the white curtains of which were carefully closed. Shot followed shot; the old wheel received two balls and gave vent to an agonizing groan; the buckets were borne off by the current; the framework was crushed. The soul of the gay mill had left it!

Then the French began the assault. There was a furious fight with swords and bayonets. Beneath the rust-colored sky the valley was choked with the dead. The broad meadows had a wild look with their tall, isolated trees and their hedges of poplars which stained them with shade. To the right and to the left the forests were like the walls of an ancient ampitheater which enclosed the fighting gladiators, while the springs, the fountains and the flowing brooks seemed to sob amid the panic of the country.

Beneath the shed Francoise still sat near Dominique's body; she had not moved. Père Merlier had received a slight wound. The Prussians were exterminated, but the ruined mill was on fire in a dozen places. The French rushed into the courtyard, headed by their captain. It was his first success of the war. His face beamed with triumph. He waved his sword, shouting:

"Victory! Victory!"

On seeing the wounded miller, who was endeavoring to comfort Francoise, and noticing the body of Dominique, his joyous look changed to one of sadness. Then he knelt beside the young man and, tearing open his blouse, put his hand to his heart.

"Thank God!" he cried. "It is yet beating! Send for the surgeon!"

At the captain's words Francoise leaped to her feet.

"There is hope!" she cried. "Oh, tell me there is hope!"

At that moment the surgeon appeared. He made a hasty examination and said:

"The young man is severely hurt, but life is not extinct; he can be saved!" By the surgeon's orders Dominique was transported to a neighboring cottage, where he was placed in bed. His wounds were dressed; restoratives were administered, and he soon recovered consciousness. When he opened his eyes he saw Francoise sitting beside him and through the open window caught sight of Père Merlier talking with the French captain. He passed his hand over his forehead with a bewildered air and said:

"They did not kill me after all!"

"No," replied Francoise. "The French came, and their surgeon saved you."

Père Merlier turned and said through the window:

"No talking yet, my young ones!"

In due time Dominique was entirely restored, and when peace again blessed the land he wedded his beloved Francoise.

The mill was rebuilt, and Père Merlier had a new wheel upon which to bestow whatever tenderness was not engrossed by his daughter and her husband.